SCHOOL

by Erica Donner

TABLE OF CONTENTS

tadpole books

SCHOOL

school

This is my school.

This is my classroom.

teacher

This is my teacher.

desk

This is my desk.

book

AROUND TOWN

FIRE STATION

tadpole books

This is my book.

pen

This is my pen.

friend

This is my friend.

WORDS TO KNOW

book

classroom

desk

friend

pen

school

INDEX